This bo

_____

Contents

Cover illustration by Tania Hurt-Newton

Published by Ladybird Books Ltd
27 Wrights Lane London W8 5TZ
A Penguin Company

2 4 6 8 10 9 7 5 3 1
© LADYBIRD BOOKS LTD MCMXCVII, MMI
LADYBIRD and the device of a Ladybird are trademarks of Ladybird Books Ltd

Printed in Italy

Now it's your turn

written by Marie Birkinshaw
illustrated by Rosslyn Moran

It was our school Sports Day.

All the mums and dads had come to watch.

OBSTACLE RACE

The green team went first.
They ran over the jumps,
under the nets and…

crash!

out went the Greens.

The mums and dads
tried hard not to laugh.

The blue team shouted,
"Now it's our turn."
And off they ran. They went
over the jumps, under the nets,
round the track and…

smash!

out went the Blues.

This time the mums and dads couldn't stop laughing.

"It must be our turn by now,"
shouted the yellow team.
They were the favourites to win.
They ran over the jumps, under
the nets, round the track, along
the wall and…

splash!

out went the Yellows.

The mums and dads were really laughing now.

"Well," said Mrs Brown, the Head Teacher. "Someone will have to win." She looked at all the mums and dads.

"So now it's **your** turn!"

The mums and dads went over the fence, through the playground and ran away to their cars.

And this time **we** had a really good laugh.

Football frenzy

written by Marie Birkinshaw
illustrated by Tania Hurt-Newton

They have Angry Anna
 and Tiger Tim.
They have Pushy Pete
 and Crashing Kim.
They have Matthew Mad
 and Gary Grim.
We really don't like
 the look of him.

They have Bouncer Ben
and Fighter Fred.
They have Lucky Lucy
and Noisy Ned.
They have Jumping James
and Giant Jed.

But they won't get the ball
round our Tiny Ted!

The school report

written by Lorraine Horsley

illustrated by Peta Blackwell

Mum came to collect me
from school.

She could see that I was worried about my school report.

She took the envelope from me and put it in her bag.

When we got home, I went up to my room.

I thought she would be angry when she read the report.

I heard her come upstairs.

"Come on, David," Mum said.
"Your dinner's getting cold!"

"It's your favourite,
chips and beans."

I said I wasn't hungry.

"Are you all right?" she asked.

"Yes," I said quietly, and
she went downstairs.

Dad came home from work.

I heard him shout up the stairs, "David, come down here, please!"

I walked very, very slowly
into the kitchen. I saw the
open envelope on the table.

"Here, read your school report,"
Dad said.

I looked at the report.
This is what it said.

School Report

MATHS   Very good work.

READING   David's reading is coming
               along very well.

SPELLING   Excellent.

SCIENCE   David likes Science.
               He works very hard.

SPORTS   David is the best runner
               in the class.

David is very helpful in class and
always tries his best. Well done.

I wasn't worried any more.

"Can I have my beans and chips now, please, Mum?"

Winding words

written by Shirley Jackson

illustrated by Justin Grassi

Read this line and you will find that round and round the words will wind. Read again and you will see that all the words wind round to me.

Winding words

Have fun following
the words as they wind
round towards the centre of
the maze. Your child will enjoy
seeing reading text presented in an unusual way.

New words

Encourage your child to use some of these new
words to write his own very simple stories
and rhymes.

Read with Ladybird

Read with Ladybird has been written to help you to help your child:

- to take the first steps in reading
- to improve early reading progress
- to gain confidence

Main Features

- **Several stories and rhymes in each book**

This means that there is not too much for you and your child to read in one go.

- **Rhyme and rhythm**

Read with Ladybird uses rhymes or stories with a rhythm to help your child to predict and memorise new words.

- **Gradual introduction and repetition of key words**

Read with Ladybird introduces and repeats the 100 most frequently used words in the English language.

- **Compatible with school reading schemes**

The key words that your child will learn are compatible with the word lists that are used in schools. This means that you can be confident that practising at home will support work done at school.

- **Information pullout**

Use this pullout to understand more about how you can use each story to help your child to learn to read.

But the most important feature of **Read with Ladybird** is for you and your child to have fun sharing the stories and rhymes with each other.